Against *All* ODDS

a novel   DISCARDED

by

PAUL KROPP

H·I·P Books

*With thanks to the Randy Anderson Learning Foundation and the students
at King Edward Academy, Edmonton, for their help in researching this book*

HIP Sr. novels

Library and Archives Canada Cataloguing in Publication

Kropp, Paul, 1948–
    Against all odds / Paul Kropp.

(New Series Canada)
ISBN 1-897039-06-9

    I. Title. II. Series.

PS8571.R772A84 2004   jC813'.54   C2004-903728-5

General editor: Paul Kropp
Text Design: Laura Brady
Illustrations redrawn by: Matt Melanson
Cover design: Robert Corrigan

2 3 4 5 6 7   07 06

Printed and bound in Canada by Webcom

High Interest Publishing is an imprint of the Chestnut Publishing group. We
acknowledge the support of the Government of Canada through the Book
Publishing Industry Development Program (BPIDP) for our publishing
activities.

Nothing ever came easy for Jeff. He had a tough time at school and hung around with all the wrong kids in the neighborhood. But when he and his brother are drowning in a storm sewer, Jeff is the one who never gives up.

CHAPTER 1

Jeff Gets Beaten Up

My little brother isn't the brightest crayon in the box. You know what I mean. I'm not saying this to put Jeff down or anything, but he's always been a bit slow. It's not that he can't do things, it just takes him longer. Sometimes it takes him a lot longer.

And sometimes he just doesn't get it, at all.

Like I've been telling him for years – stay away from Tank. Tank is the bully around this part of

Edmonton. He's got a real name, Tankowicz or something like that, but we all call him Tank. Like most bullies, he's a bit crazy. I think his old man must have dropped him on his head, but who really knows? Tank likes to pick on kids. He won't get near me, but he picks on kids who are smaller or dumber than he is.

Anybody with half a brain would just stay clear of a guy like that. You don't have to be a rocket scientist to figure it out. You just stay away. The bully is on one side of the street, you get on the other. KISS – keep it simple, stupid.

That's just what I told Jeff, my little brother. "If you don't hang around with Tank, he won't bother you." I must have said it a hundred times.

So what does the kid do? Jeff goes off and hangs around with the Tank and his scummy friends. Like I said, my brother isn't the brightest crayon in the box. So maybe I shouldn't have been surprised when he came in like he did. My little brother was a mess.

"What happened to you?" I asked.

He just stood there wiping his nose, but the

story was written all over him. He had a bloody nose, a ripped shirt and no jacket. Dirt covered his hands and face. He looked like he'd been in a fight with a truck and come out second best.

"They hit me," he said.

"Who's they?" I snapped back.

"My friends."

"Some friends," I said with a snarl. "It was Tank and his guys, right? How many times have I told you not to hang out with them?"

"Yeah, but –"

"Yeah but nothing," I said, cutting him off. "You get a new Oilers jacket and right away those punks want to grab it from you."

"They borrowed it," Jeff said, as if he really believed that. "Tank will make the guy give it back."

"Yeah, right. Those guys have about two days to bring it back or they'll be dealing with me and the cops – in that order." This was the kind of thing that always got me so angry. Now my brother was sitting there, no jacket, beaten up. How could I let that kind of thing keep going on?

"So how did you get roughed up?" I asked him.

"Were you hanging out in the storm sewers again?"

"Yeah, but don't tell Mom, please, Larry?"

I shook my head. The storm sewers were maybe the stupidest place to hang out. They're really big sewer pipes, almost big enough to stand up in. They run under and around our neighbourhood, going down to Mill Creek. Most of the time they're dry as a bone, or maybe with a little bit of water at the bottom. But when a storm hits, they're killers. Water pours into them from the streets and storm drains. If you're in the sewers, the water can wash you right into the river.

And that's if you're lucky.

I knew Tank and his gang made the sewers their clubhouse. They used them for some stupid games – like hide-and-seek, only dumber. It also gave them a place to scare the little kids. What better way to steal lunch money than tell a kid he'll be trapped in a sewer? I mean, it's worth fifty cents just to avoid the trouble.

"Listen, Jeff," I began, "we've got to have a talk, a serious talk."

"Yeah, I know," Jeff replied, looking guilty as

anything. "Let me go get cleaned up first. My swimming is … like, five o'clock."

So what could I say? My brother needed to get the blood off, and he did have a swim team practice at Queen Elizabeth Pool in about half an hour. Of course, it was my job to drive him. I got my licence about two months ago, but I drive Jeff around more than I drive myself. Still, it takes some pressure off Mom and Dad, and I get to use the new SUV when I'm taking Jeff someplace. My parents think the big SUV is safer than our old Chevy. Just goes to show how much they know.

Jeff got cleaned up while I found his gym bag up in his room. I did the kid a real favour. I traded a dry bathing suit for the wet one he'd left in the bag.

My brother isn't too smart about clothes and friends, but he's a great swimmer. Really, he might make the city team if he takes a couple of seconds off his hundred-metre crawl. But Jeff doesn't stop to think about throwing his wet suit in the dryer. Sometimes I think his mind is on some other planet.

It took Jeff ten minutes to get cleaned up. Then he spent another ten minutes packing his stuff. At last, we got into the car and drove down Whyte Avenue, a bit faster than we should have.

"Are you mad, Larry?" my brother asked me.

"Yeah, I'm mad. You're stupid to hang out with those guys and stupid to play in the sewers. It serves you right that they stole your jacket."

"Mom said you're not supposed to call me stupid," Jeff replied. He seemed a little hurt by the word, or maybe he was just pretending. And he was right, really, but I didn't want to admit that.

"Anybody else who calls you stupid, I'll kill him," I replied. "But I'll call you stupid when you do something stupid, like hanging out with Tank. So stop, that's all I'm saying."

"They're my friends," he replied.

"They're not your *friends*!" I shot back. "They're just using you. They steal your clothes, take your lunch money and make fun of you. Today, they beat you up. That's not friends, that's nutbars."

"Yeah, yeah, I know," he replied.

"So promise me you'll stay away from them.

There are lots of decent guys to hang out with. That guy Evan in your class – he's okay, maybe a little weird, but okay. Go play some video games with Evan. Go hang out with the guys on your swim team. Just remember, Tank and his guys are bad news."

Jeff said nothing.

"Besides, I don't feel like having to scrape your body off a sewer grate some day. Just stay away from trouble."

"You're right, Larry," he told me. "You're always right."

But Jeff didn't promise me a thing.

CHAPTER 2

Tough Guy

Two days later, I was walking home from school. I was walking with Megan, who is not, let me add, a girlfriend. She's a friend friend, but maybe someday down the line ... well, who knows? She's cool and smart and popular – a lot of things I'm not. But never mind. We were talking about Egghead Ebert's math class, or something like that, when I heard a bunch of yelling.

"Kids," I grunted, paying no attention.

"Sounds like one of them is in trouble," Megan replied.

We could both hear the sound of crying and a kind of high-pitched moaning. The sound was muffled a little because it was from the tunnels, way off to the left. The kid who was crying might be drowning in the sewers for all we could tell.

"Maybe you should go check it out," Megan suggested.

Most other times, I would have shrugged and kept on going. Kids playing in the storm sewers – nothing new about that. But when a good-looking blonde looks into your eyes and says, "Maybe you should go check it out," well, that's what you do.

What choice did I have? I left Megan standing on the sidewalk and went over to the open part of the sewer. Nothing. In the distance, where the sewer went under the street, I could hear more shouting. It was dark in that part, so I couldn't see much even when I looked hard. I was thinking about walking in there to see what the problem was, but the "problem" came running out towards me.

It was Jeff.

"Oh, holy …" I swore under my breath.

There was blood dripping from his nose and a wild look in his eyes. His hair was standing up on end, and his clothes were so dirty, you'd think he had been rolling in the mud.

Jeff stopped cold when he saw me. He looked back over his shoulder, then down at his feet. It was as if Jeff were hoping that I was some kind of a bad dream, that I really wasn't there.

"Jeff, what –" I began, but my words were cut off.

A kid named Rocco came running out of the dark tunnel. He was wearing Jeff's Oilers jacket. Rocco blinked for a second from the bright light, and then he saw Jeff. A second later, he saw me.

Maybe there was something about the look on my face, but Rocco just froze. He put this phony smile on his face, a look that said, *we're just kids having some fun.*

I didn't buy it.

"Okay, goof," I said, going over to Rocco, "what's going on?" I grabbed the kid by the neck. That was bad, but I admit it. I have a bit of a temper, and sometimes it comes out. When I saw Rocco chasing my brother, wearing Jeff's jacket, I kind of lost it.

"We were …" Rocco began, but he had a hard time talking, with my fingers digging into his neck.

"Let him go!" Jeff shouted. "Let him go!"

Then I heard a girl's voice coming down from up above us all. "Larry, isn't that a little too much strong-arm stuff? He's just a kid."

Megan was right, of course. Rocco was only thirteen or fourteen, the same age as Jeff. He was younger and way smaller than me. I was mad, all

right, but that didn't make it fair for me to strangle the kid.

"Give me the jacket!" I said, looking the little jerk right in the eye.

"Yeah, yeah," he said, stripping it off as fast as anything.

"It's okay, Larry, Rocco just borrowed it," my brother said.

I ignored him and kept on. I took the Oilers jacket in one hand, then used my finger to pound Rocco in the chest.

"I want to see Tank – out here – in five minutes. Got it? Five minutes or I'm coming in … and I won't be a happy camper."

Rocco turned on his heels and ran into the tunnel. That left three of us standing around in the sunshine, just outside the entrance to the storm sewer. Megan had jumped down and given Jeff a Kleenex.

"What's going on?" I snapped at my brother.

"We were playing this game …" he began.

"Yeah, nice game," I told him, staring at his ripped clothes. "So who was doing the crying in there? Anybody I know?"

"We were just having fun," Jeff whined.

I was mad, mad as anything. I could feel the blood pumping through my veins, my heart beating like crazy, my hands clenching and unclenching. It was always like this. Jeff was three years younger than me. It felt like I'd spent my whole life protecting him.

Back in elementary school, kids would mock him or pull his hair. But I'd be in there – fast as anything. So maybe I was as stupid as they were, but nobody was going to pick on my brother. Nobody was going to make fun of him or his problem.

So I became a kind of bully myself. *Touch my brother and I'll thump you.* That was what I told people and it's what I did.

I remember once, in grade five, some kid called my brother a retard. "What did you say?" I asked the kid. He repeated the word, like it meant nothing at all, and I could feel my back tense up. I grabbed the kid, right at the neck, and held him up against a wall until he was red in the face. "What did you say?" I repeated. The kid could barely talk, but at last he coughed an apology: "Nothing, I didn't say nothing."

Sure, I got in trouble. I was given detentions and sent home and even suspended once. But after a while the word got out – you pick on Jeff and his big brother will be on your case.

"Larry, you've got to calm down," Megan told me. "It's no big deal. You got the jacket back and now it's all over. Let's go back to my house and hang out."

I should have said yes. Any guy with half a brain

would have said yes. A pretty girl – a girl I liked – had just invited me to her place after school. I'd been waiting for a chance like this for months, but I was ready to throw it all away.

"Megan, I've got to deal with this," I told her. I looked at my watch. "That bum has two minutes to come back with Tank or I'm going in there."

"What are you going to do?" Megan snapped back. "Beat them all up? Sometimes you act like you're about five years old."

With that Megan turned and climbed back up to the street. I looked up at her, a thin shadow with the sun behind her.

"Jeff, you look after your big brother," she called down. "Sometimes I think Larry's too dumb for his own good."

Jeff giggled as Megan walked away, disappearing from our view.

"She called you dumb, Larry. She said you were dumb, not me."

I shook my head and looked off into the dark tunnel. "Yeah, well, it's all a matter of opinion. It's been five minutes and I don't see your buddies out here. You think Tank is hiding from me?"

My brother smiled again, as if I'd made a big joke. "Maybe he is – that's our game."

"Yeah, swell game," I snapped back. "Let's go find him."

It was four o'clock on a sunny, cloud-free afternoon. We went into the tunnel – my brother first, me second – and put the world of light and air behind us.

CHAPTER 3

In the Sewer

Let me tell you a few things about storm sewers. First, they're dark, a little small and smelly. Even a big storm sewer is only a couple metres tall. The small branch lines are so small you could wedge your shoulders in them and never get out. Second – this is the good news – a storm sewer only handles rainwater. The stuff you flush down a toilet or the muck that goes down your sink, that goes off through some other sewer. A storm sewer is only for rainwater, or flood water, depending. It also gets street dirt, motor oil and more than a little dog crap, which explains the smell.

Most of the time, though, there's not much water in the sewer. There's a little stream that goes down the centre, but it's not big enough to get your feet wet. There are little ledges on both sides, anyway. You can get up a little even if the water flow gets a bit heavy.

When I was a kid, I used to play down in the storm sewers. I figured the system out pretty quick. Mostly the storm sewers go under the street, from catch basin to catch basin, manhole to manhole. Sometimes they join up to a bigger line. The big lines have water all the time. They end with big grates to stop branches and dead animals from washing into the river. I never went into the big storm sewer lines. I mean, I can be dumb and take chances, but I'm not a fool.

For the life of me, I can't figure out why guys would hang out in a storm sewer. You can play a game or two, maybe chase or tag or hide-and-seek. But there are only so many places to hide and it's easy to get lost. Besides, they stink! They're sewers, after all.

But here we were, Jeff and me, making our way through the dark. With each step I took, I felt a little more stupid. What was I doing here, anyhow? What was I trying to prove?

"So where do your friends hang out?" I asked.

"Not far," Jeff replied, "unless they're hiding. Then we've got to find them!"

His voice was smiling. It was as if this was all some kind of game.

"Here, put your jacket on," I told him. "It's as cold as a walk-in fridge down here."

We kept moving forward through the sewer tunnel. I've got a little problem with closed-in places, and that got worse with each step. Over our heads was dirt, under our feet was a little stream of water, and all around us was darkness. This was like some Stephen King story. I kept expecting to get trapped by something. I kept waiting for something to jump out at us.

"How much farther?" I asked.

"Just ahead, round the corner," Jeff replied.

That worked for me. There was a little light up ahead. I could see a catch basin that let in some daylight. Human beings, like us, we have this thing for light. It makes us feel good. Sewers are for water and dead things, not for us. No wonder I wanted out, but quick.

Up ahead, there was a little bright spot in the gloom. It was a reminder that the sun was still shining. Someplace. Someplace not here.

We heard a noise. It sounded like a rat running on concrete. Except that we don't have rats in Edmonton. So maybe it was Tank and his gang moving from place to place.

"Hey," I called out. "Hey, Tank. I want to talk to you."

There was no reply, no voices, no movement.

"Your friends don't want to talk to me," I said to Jeff.

"They're hiding," my brother told me. "We're all scared of you."

Did my brother say *we're* or *they're*? It was all so strange down in the sewers. Sound seemed to bounce around from all over. Voices and squeaks sounded bigger in the tunnels. And then there was the sound of water, dripping water, always the water.

"All right, Tank, stop playing games," I shouted. The words bounced around the sewer, then back at me. *Games-games-games.* "I've got something to say to you!" *You-you-you.*

There was a sound in the darkness, a whisper, then more sounds. People were moving around us, beside us, above us. But that was impossible – there was no room.

"Tank!" I shouted. My voice was very high, and my throat pinched.

More noises, and then a reply.

"You called?" asked the voice. A flashlight flipped on and a beam of light shot up at Tank's fat face. In the dark, at that angle, his face looked like the mask of a dead man.

I jumped back, frightened just a bit, and hit my head against the top of the tunnel.

"Better be careful, Larry," Tank said. "You don't know your way down here."

Then another voice came from the side. "But we do."

The flashlight moved to point at me, and I was blinded. For a second, we all froze in the tunnel. Except for our breathing and a drip of water

somewhere, it was quiet. I was shaking a little, so I reached to touch one wall.

Tank broke the silence. "You're a little shaky, Larry. Maybe you should just leave – that is, if you can remember how you got here to begin with."

They laughed, all of them, maybe at the look on my face. *This is getting out of control*, I told myself. I had come down to lay down the law. I had come down here to keep them from bugging my brother. Now I was scared out of my head and looking like a fool.

"Listen," I began, "I just want you guys to leave my brother alone." I tried to sound tough, like I was the guy in charge. But my voice was high and seemed to end with a question mark. *Alone-alone-alone.*

"Maybe your brother doesn't want to be left alone, Larry," Tank replied. "Maybe he likes us better than he likes you."

There was more laughter and then the flashlight went off. In the darkness, I could hear running shoes hitting against the concrete. These little guys were running off, hiding in tunnels so small I'd never find them. Then there was only silence around us – silence and my own breathing.

I swore – at them and at myself. Then I turned to where my brother had been. "Okay, Jeff, let's get out of here."

No reply. I reached out in the darkness to grab him, but my hand touched nothing but air.

"Jeff … Jeff?"

There was more laughter way down in the tunnel somewhere.

"Jeff, how do we get out of here?" I asked, and then screamed. "We've got to get out of here!"

CHAPTER 4

Think It Through

I got out okay, once I could get my head straight. There was still that little point of light that I remembered, so I just walked out towards the light. It's funny how easy it is to get lost when you're under pressure and a little scared. All I had to do was calm down and I was just fine.

Jeff came home a little later, then went off to a swimming practice with Mom before I could ask him anything. When I talked to him the next day, he said that the whole thing was a game. He laughed and acted as if it was all so cool, so I had to act as if it were just a laugh for me, too.

But I didn't like it. I didn't like how this was shaping up at all.

"So what's your problem?" Megan asked me.

We were sitting at our school's basketball game. Our team was losing badly, but that didn't matter much. I'd take any excuse to spend time with Megan, even sitting in the bleachers to watch a hopeless game.

"It's *my* problem?" I asked. We had been talking about my brother and Tank's little gang.

"Yeah, maybe it is," she told me. Megan turned toward me, pushed a little blonde hair off her face and smiled. She has a nice smile. It's enough to cover up some pretty tough ideas.

"Like how?"

"Your brother doesn't have a problem," she told me. "He's made some friends, has a little fun, and maybe you don't like what they do, but so what? Your parents don't seem too worried about it, so what's the big deal?"

"I just don't like it when people take advantage of Jeff. You know he's got a few problems, like he's not the brightest crayon in the box –"

"I've heard you say that before, Larry, and it's not very nice."

"But it's true. The kid is more like a child than a thirteen-year-old. Guys like Tank make fun of him and Jeff doesn't even know it."

"If he doesn't know it, then there's no problem," Megan said quietly.

"Yeah, that's like saying our basketball team

doesn't have a problem so long as they don't look at the score."

She grinned at me. "That's a good one, Larry – no wonder you always get straight A's. But I'm still wondering why you have such a problem with this Tank guy."

My answer came pretty quick. "Look, playing games in storm sewers just isn't safe. A big storm, a flash flood, and those guys are as dead as those people at the end of *Titanic*. That could be my brother who ends up drowned."

"Good point," she said. "Your parents should talk to Jeff and make sure he understands that. But there's got to be more to it, Larry."

I started to squirm in my seat. Talking to Megan was like talking to a shrink. You'd say something reasonable, and she'd start picking for more. And there really was a little more.

It was seven or eight years ago, when we were all little kids. Tank and I are the same age and, back then, we were about the same size. He lived about two houses away from us then, and we used to play together the way kids do. Tank wasn't so much a bully back then, either. He was a short, stocky kid, but I called him by his real name, Tommy.

One day we were playing outside, some game of lasers and falling dead, and I was supposed to be looking after Jeff. My parents had gone off to the mall for a bit and left me in charge. I felt pretty grown-up, even though I was all of eight or nine years old.

Anyway, Tank and I were playing and Jeff kept wanting to join in. He was only five or six years old, but he acted a lot younger. "Me play! Me play!" he'd shout. But it took a long time to explain a game to Jeff, and then he'd mess it up. I used to get pretty embarrassed about that, about how much trouble he'd have with a stupid little game.

"Let your brother play," Tank said.

"Me play!" Jeff agreed.

So I went along with it. We tried to keep the game going, but Jeff kept on dying too soon. Or he'd shoot his laser into the sky and wait for us to fall dead. He just didn't get it.

"Your brother's a real dummy, ain't he?" Tank said.

"Don't call him a dummy," I shot back. "He does the best he can."

"Yeah, well, he's still a dummy."

"I told you not to say that word."

As you could predict, we got into a fight. It was a little-kid fight, lots of pushing and kicking and punches that didn't connect. But then I fell down, and Tank got on top of me and started punching my head. That's what my parents saw when they pulled into the drive.

So little Tommy – Tank – wasn't welcome at our house after that. And I wasn't trusted to look after my brother for a couple of years.

I decided that nothing like that would happen to me again. I began working out in my parents' home gym. At the same time, I started growing taller. By the time I was twelve, there was no way I'd ever lose a fight to Tank again. But it didn't mean I ever forgave him for that day.

That's what I told Megan, all of it.

"So now it makes sense," she said. "You don't like your brother hanging out with the kid who beat you up, like, eight years ago."

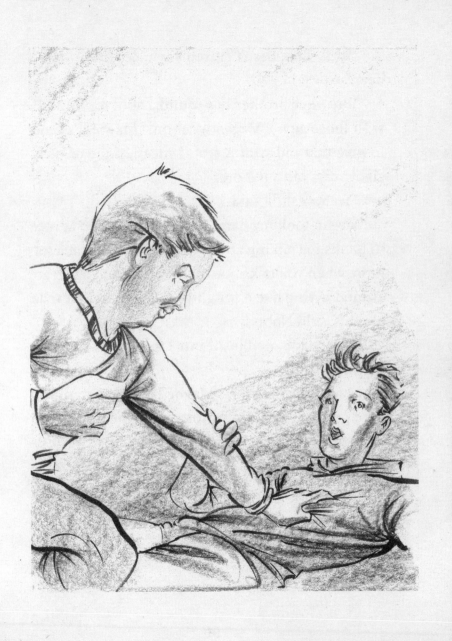

"Well, Tank hasn't gotten any nicer from what I hear."

"But your brother has found a spot for himself with those guys," Megan went on. "Maybe it's time to give that old stuff a rest. I mean, none of us is eight years old anymore."

"Yeah, yeah," I said.

Megan took my hand in hers and smiled at me. "Thanks for talking about it, Larry. I like you a lot more when you talk about things than when you go around acting like a tough guy. You're not all that tough, really. Nobody is."

That made me blush, but I kept holding onto Megan's hand.

Maybe she was right. Maybe I'd spent too much time protecting my little brother. Maybe it was time to let Jeff start protecting himself.

CHAPTER 5

I'm Going In!

After talking to Megan, I started to see things a little differently. My little brother really was growing up. He had his own life, his own swim team, his own friends. The special classes at school had done a lot for him. Jeff got on just fine with most of the kids at school. His reading was pretty good and his math got better all the time. Sure, things came kind of slow to him. The stuff I could get in a flash, he'd have to work at for ages.

But so what? There are guys who get advanced math in a flash, and it takes me ages to figure that stuff out. I guess brainpower is all relative. And maybe it's not all that important, in the big picture.

So I tried to ease up. I talked to my parents about Jeff playing in the storm sewers. They talked to him about being careful, and what might happen. That was that – not my problem anymore.

Besides, I had my own life to live. This thing with Megan was getting pretty serious. We were hanging out all the time now, and the kids at school all thought we were hooking up. Well, I wish. But still, we spent a lot of time together and that was more than fine by me.

We were walking to her place after school that day in May. There were rain clouds hanging over our heads, dark and heavy, ready to soak us both. Megan was showing me her new cellphone. It's one of those phones that takes pictures, sends text and somehow clicks onto the Internet. You can see all this on a tiny little screen, about the size of two thumbnails.

"Watch this," Megan said, clicking away with her fingers.

In a second, she had Internet weather up on the screen, with STORM WARNING in letters that filled the screen.

"See, this tells you that you might need an umbrella – " and then she stopped cold. We were both thinking exactly the same thing – *where was Jeff?*

"Better call my house," I said, trying to keep my voice calm.

A quick click of the memory button and the phone rang at my house. It rang once, twice, three times and then the answering voice cut in.

My first word was a curse, and then I added some explanation. "Jeff's in the storm sewers."

The two of us began running. The storm sewers were right under our feet, but the only way into them was two blocks to the east, near the ravine. We were out of breath when we reached the entrance. One look told me more than I wanted to know.

Jeff's coat – the Oilers jacket – was lying at one side.

"That stupid –" I began.

"Stop it," Megan lectured me. "Bad-mouthing your brother isn't going to help. I'm going to phone for help. If Jeff is down there, so are the others. They've got to get out before the storm hits or they'll be in real trouble."

She began punching 911 into the phone while I scrambled down into the sewer. There was my brother's jacket, as dirty as the day I got it back from Rocco. In front of me was the sewer entrance. There was a grate that the kids had pulled off, so now there was just a black tunnel leading under the streets.

A tunnel leading to death.

I could hear Megan's voice up above, talking to the 911 person. I climbed into the tunnel and shouted: "A storm is coming! You've got to get out!" There was no answer, just the echo of my words. *Out-out-out.*

I shouted again, and then a third time.

"Jeff!" I cried.

The water beneath my feet was just a trickle; it wouldn't even get a running shoe very wet. But

once the rain started, this little trickle could turn into a flood. It took no time at all.

I pulled back from the tunnel, then looked up at Megan. "Nothing," I said to her.

"They're going to send somebody," Megan shouted down. "There's some problem downtown, some kind of flooding, so it might be a while."

I heard a clap of thunder and felt the first drops of rain begin to fall. The clouds were black now, a thunderstorm ready to dump a sky full of water onto the streets of the city. Then the streets would dump it all into the storm sewers. With luck, Jeff would see the water rising and get out while he still could. With luck, Tank and his buddies would make sure my little brother got out. With luck.

And then there was me. I could sit out here and wait – wait for my brother, wait for the cops. Or I could grit my teeth and do something. It didn't take long to make up my mind.

"I'm going in," I shouted to Megan. "You stay here and tell the police."

"That's stupid," she screamed. "You could get killed."

"Don't use that word," I yelled, as I ran into the sewer opening.

CHAPTER 6

In the Tunnel

I ducked and headed into the tunnel. I was under the street now, making my way in from the open sewer. At first, there was still enough light to see. But after twenty steps, I was deep in gloom. Behind me, back where I had come in, was a circle of light leading outside, where Megan was waiting for the police. Ahead of me was blackness.

"Jeff!" I shouted out, but only echoes came back to me. *Jeff-Jeff-Jeff.*

Then there was another sound, a crack and roar of thunder as the storm outside let go. The rumble of thunder bounced around the concrete, maybe worse than it was outside.

"Jeff!" I yelled again.

From somewhere deep in the tunnel, I heard something, or I thought I did. Was it a voice?

I splashed forward. The water at my feet had turned into a little stream. Fed by the storm outside, the water flowed past my feet, down into the tunnel. Someplace up ahead, somewhere, the stream would burst out of the sewers into Mill Creek. If I didn't get out in time, the stream would carry me – or my body – along with it.

"Jeff, where are you?" I called out as I moved forward.

This time I thought I heard something like *over here*, but I couldn't be sure.

I kept going into the darkness. Beneath me, the water was splashing over my ankles. It had soaked my running shoes and the bottom of my jeans, and now it was up over my ankles. How long had I been in here? If the water had gone up this much in five minutes, how long before it would be at my waist? How long before it would fill the tunnel and I'd be a dead man?

"Larry?"

That stopped my mental math. This time I was sure it was a voice calling my name. It had to be my brother. I didn't know where he was or how long it would take me to get there, but I knew it was his voice.

"Jeff, where are you?" I shouted off into the darkness.

Some kind of answer came back, but it was lost in the rush of the water and the echoes in the tunnel.

"Tell me again ... slow!" I screamed, trying to talk slowly myself.

I've had nightmares like this – about being trapped in the darkness, screaming, lost. In the nightmares I'm fighting against something, or something is grabbing me. I struggle against the darkness and the cold. I have to fight against the thing that's grabbing me. Sometimes I get pulled down and can't breathe. Sometimes I fight against the thing and just wake up in a sweat.

But this was no dream. This was real life, and my brother was trapped someplace in the tunnel.

"Go forward, then go right," I heard. The voice was far away, blurred by distance and the echoes.

"Forward, right, are you sure?" I called back, even as I splashed forward.

Jeff was never good with directions, the left/right thing. If I made a wrong turn in this darkness, I'd never find him.

"That's right," I heard, but it was a different voice.

How many of them were there? I asked myself.

By now I was so far into the tunnel that I couldn't see the light behind me. Or maybe the storm had made it pitch black outside, so there was no light. I was trapped under the sidewalk, lost and blind.

And then the terror hit me. I thought about where I was, the darkness and the water. I thought about dying. In a flash, I thought about how stupid this was and how hopeless. I knew I was losing it, and had to fight back.

Get a grip, I told myself. *Make a plan.*

The plan was simple – keep moving forward until I found them, then lead them back out. Maybe it wasn't a great plan, but it seemed okay at the moment. I tried to work through the details, like how much time we had. I tried to focus on the plan and not the terror. If I let my mind snap back to being trapped in the tunnel and its darkness, I'd be frozen to the spot. So I didn't think, I just kept moving.

"I'm coming!" I called out.

"You're getting closer," I heard. It was Jeff's voice for sure.

"Can you come towards me?" I shouted. Now that made sense. If we were going to go back the way I had come in, why weren't they coming my way?

"We're stuck," Jeff called.

That made no sense to me. How could anybody get stuck in a concrete tunnel? But at that moment

I reached the tunnel going off to the right – and my nightmare got worse.

It was smaller! To get through it, I'd have to crawl on my hands and knees.

"Are you down here?" I yelled.

"Not far," Jeff said. "There's air here."

What did he mean by that?

I climbed into the tunnel and crawled forward. *Don't think about where you are,* I told myself. Don't think about the darkness and the water and getting trapped down here. Just don't think.

"How far?" I cried.

"Almost here," Jeff called back. "Be care …"

I didn't hear the end of the word. Suddenly I was slipping forward, falling into the darkness. The water under my knees was all around me and I had to fight to breathe.

It was like falling into a wave pool, getting pushed by the water so you're just out of control. There was no sense swimming, no sense fighting it. I was being washed away, like a guy drowning in a flood, so all I could do was hold my breath.

But then, just as quickly as I had gone under,

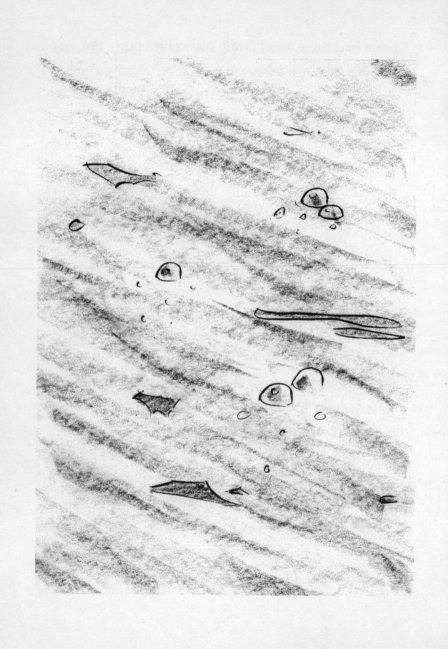

my head came up and I was gasping for air.

I took a quick breath and then a deep one. In the gloom, I saw a couple of points of light way up over my head. Then, in the reflected light, I saw two bodies.

CHAPTER 7

Did You Bring Help?

One of the bodies moved, and then it spoke, "So did you bring help?"

"Help?" I replied. For a split second I wasn't sure whether I was saying help or asking for help.

"Yeah, you brought somebody with you, right?" I heard. It was Tank, one of the black shapes in the gloom.

"I told you Larry would save us," Jeff spoke up. He was the other shape in this tiny space.

"I . . . uh, well, Megan's called the police," I explained.

"So you just came in by yourself?" Tank said. "That's real smart, Larry. You come in to play hero and you don't even have a plan or anybody to back you up?"

He was right, of course. I hadn't had much of a plan when I went charging into the storm sewer. I didn't even know the way back out now that I was down here. The small tunnel must have turned down at some point, and I had been washed along it. Now we were all in some sort of place where the little tunnel dumped into a bigger one. The cold water was up to my waist, and I was standing on a side ledge. If I stepped off, the water would be up to my chest.

"You guys have any idea where we are?" I asked.

"I dunno, Larry," Tank said. "I was looking for a street sign, but it's kind of dark. You didn't happen to bring a flashlight with you, or maybe a cellphone? I mean, that would have required a little brainpower." Tank was making fun of me, just the way he used to when we were little.

My brother didn't even notice Tank's words. "Larry's got a light on his key chain," Jeff blurted out.

Why hadn't I thought about that? I was supposed to be the smart one, and it was my brother who figured that out.

"Yeah, I've got a little flashlight," I said, feeling pretty dumb. I reached into my soaking jeans and pulled out my keys. The flashlight was as wet as the rest of me, but it turned on. For the first time in maybe ten minutes, my eyes saw something besides black.

"What kind of place is this?" I said. I was moving the beam all around – on Jeff and Tank and the concrete walls.

Way up over our heads I could see a couple points of light. It looked like a big metal plate up there, with a couple holes that let in some daylight.

"It must be where the side sewer connects to the main line," Tank explained. "That's a manhole cover up there."

We were about five metres down in the sewer,

waist-deep in water, but just over our heads was a way out.

"So why didn't you guys climb out?" I asked.

"It's locked," my brother told me.

"The city locked it down 'cause, well, one day we kind of left it off," Tank explained. "We went up and tried pushing already, but the thing is stuck or locked." At least he was talking to me straight, now.

"So let's hit the thing and make some noise," I told them. I flashed the beam around the sewer, looking for something metal that I could pound on the manhole cover.

"Jeff, give me your belt."

"My belt?" he asked.

"Just take it off and give it to me," I ordered.

In a second I had my brother's belt in my hand and I was going up the metal rungs. It was only fifteen rungs to the top, and I got there fast. Jeff kept the flashlight aimed on me as I climbed up.

First, I tried to do what they had – I pushed on the manhole cover. Not a budge. I read somewhere that manhole covers weigh as much as I do, but this one was locked down tight. There was no way

I could push it open, so I decided to make some noise.

I began whapping the cover with Jeff's belt. One – two – three, and the belt buckle made the iron ring out.

"Hey, we're down here!" I yelled through the two small holes in the cover.

All we needed was one person to walk by and hear. All we needed was one person to say, "Hey, there's something funny down there." But there was no answer from up above.

I kept hitting against the cover, again and again, and yelling as often as I could. "Help!" I shouted. "We need help down here!"

Why couldn't anybody hear? I asked myself. *Where were Megan and the cops?*

Then I heard a noise, like a whoosh and a roar, and the manhole cover moved, and then the roar went away.

A car just ran over the manhole cover, I said to myself. *We are under the middle of the street!*

That's when I really started to swear. Nobody was going to hear me pounding in the middle of the street. In the storm outside, no one would even be on the sidewalks. There was nobody to hear me shouting or hitting at the metal cover.

"You shouldn't swear, Larry," my brother said.

"That's right, Larry," Tank repeated. I didn't know if he was making fun of Jeff or me or both of us, but Tank was the least of our problems.

"Yeah, you're right," I said, climbing down the rungs. "Let's forget that one."

When I got back to the bottom, there was worse news waiting for me. The water in the main sewer line had gone up. Now it was as high as Jeff's chest. That meant it had gone up half a metre in only five minutes or so. If it kept going up, we'd be forced to climb up into the manhole tube just to breathe. And if it *still* kept going up, we'd run out of air.

"Can we get back out that side tunnel?" I asked.

"Too slippery," Tank replied. "We already tried and got washed down here, just like you."

"What about the main line here?" I asked.

The water in the big tunnel was rushing by us, like a real river. It was swirling and bubbling, with dirt and branches floating on the surface. All the junk from the street was washing down to where we were.

"It goes down to Mill Creek," Tank said.

"So how about we go with the flow?" I suggested. "Jeff's a good swimmer and there's enough air at the top of the tunnel. If we wait, the water will fill the whole sewer and we'll never make it."

"Yeah, maybe you guys can make it," Tank said, "but I can't swim."

CHAPTER 8

The Wave

You can guess what was going through my mind. Jeff and I really could make it – I was sure of that. Maybe Tank could just look after himself. It wasn't my fault that the kid didn't know how to swim. It wasn't my fault that we were trapped down here, five metres below the road. It wasn't my fault that these fools were playing in the sewers just when a storm hit.

All I wanted was to keep my brother and me

alive. I just wanted to get out of here before the water got so high that we'd drown.

"Don't do it, Larry," Tank said. It was as if he were reading my mind.

"Don't do what?" I asked.

"Don't leave me here while you two go off," he said. "I don't want to die in here all by myself ..." His voice trailed off.

I flashed the light on his face. Tank was wet, soaked, just like all of us. His T-shirt was plastered to his body, showing all the muscles. Tank had always been a big guy, my height, but with real muscles where all I had were string bean arms and legs. That's why he could beat me up back when we were eight or nine years old. That's why he ended up with half my lunch money, until the day I learned to stand up to him.

Now he was freezing down here in the sewer. His muscles were useless against the water that was rushing by us. What good was all that strength if he couldn't swim?

"We could bring help," I said.

"Help is coming," Tank said. "You said your

girlfriend called the cops. So just wait here with me, okay? Just don't leave me here alone." His voice was awful, like that of a scared little kid.

That's when Jeff spoke up. "We're not going to leave you behind," he said. "Larry wouldn't do that and I wouldn't do that. You're my best buddy, you know."

"So the big, tough guy is scared, eh?" I asked, looking at him.

"Not scared of you, reject," he snapped back at me.

"You two stop," my brother said, his voice cracking with tears or anger or both. "We're going to get out of here – all of us – we just have to wait for somebody to find us."

"Yeah, well, somebody did find us, but that's done a lot of good so far," Tank muttered.

I kept my mouth shut and tried to think. Megan had called the police and they had to be coming. Somebody had to be trying to find us. But how long had it been? It felt as if I'd been in the tunnel for hours, but it must have only been ten or fifteen minutes.

I aimed the flashlight down on my watch and tried to figure. It read 4:42. I was talking to Megan at maybe four o'clock when we saw the storm warning, so we'd been in the storm sewer for about forty minutes. The water had gone from nothing to waist-high in forty minutes. So I should be able to figure…. But my brain wasn't working. A simple math problem and I just couldn't figure it.

Get control of yourself and think, I told myself.

Okay, my waist is about halfway on my body. So if the water was up that far in forty minutes then … then we'd be dead by 5:30.

I shivered in the cold water, maybe from the temperature, maybe from my simple math. They say that when you're going to die, your whole life passes before your eyes. Well, mine didn't. I kept looking around the tunnel, trying to find some way out.

From the manhole up above, we could hear the siren of a cop car. I could only hope that they were coming for us. I had to hope they had some kind of sewer map and could figure this out. The water was rising higher each second and was now up to the

level of my chest. I looked at my watch: 4:50. We wouldn't even make it to five o'clock the way the water was rising.

"Listen, I've got an idea," I said. "Tank can go up under the manhole – that will give him a little more air – and then Jeff and I will take off and go for help."

Tank shook his head. "I told you, I can't do it, Larry. I'll freak out and go nuts. When they get back and find my body, you'll know that you're the guy who left me behind."

"The water is coming up faster," I told him. "We can't all get up there, but there's room in the manhole shaft for one guy. That's gotta be you, Tank."

"No way," Tank screamed. "No way I'm dying here like some rat in a sewer! Listen, Larry, I'm begging you … I can't go like that."

"We're all going to die the way it is now," I shouted.

"No," my brother screamed. "We're not going to die! Tank, we're not going to let you die, either. I promise."

Over our heads, we could hear a massive clap of thunder. The water began roaring faster and faster around our bodies.

"Hold on!" I screamed.

We jammed our fingers into the concrete, holding on as best we could. The water around our bodies was slamming into us, like the wave at the Fantasyland wave pool, only it didn't stop. My chest and head kept getting hit with branches, pop cans, water bottles and other junk from the street.

And then, in the dim light, I saw the wave coming.

CHAPTER 9

Forty-Five Seconds

It came with a roar. Suddenly there was a wall of water filling the whole tunnel. It came at us so fast that there was no time to get ready.

"We're going – " I began, but there wasn't enough time to say *under*. There was only enough time to grab a breath and get under the surface of the water.

Even under water, the force of the wave knocked and pushed us around like crazy. It was like getting swamped at the wave pool, but the storm sewer was only a little bigger than we were. When the wave hit, we were tossed, twirled and thrown against the rough sides of the tunnel. The concrete scraped against my shoulders and legs, but there was nothing we could do. There was no way we could fight the force of the water.

For a second, I thought it was all over. We were being swept through the tunnel as fast as a car along a city street. There was no air to breathe, nothing to cling to. The future was clear – death when our lungs gave out.

Forty-five seconds

At some point, I remembered that number. It went back to the swimming lessons that Jeff and I had taken at Queen Elizabeth Pool. We used to do this thing they called the deadman's float. The idea was to hold your breath as long as you could. Jeff was the best, of course. He could hold his breath for a minute, maybe longer. Once he held his breath so long that the lifeguard jumped in to pull him out. Jeff just laughed when the lifeguard put her arm around his neck. He'd fooled us all. But that's how I knew that I could hold my breath for forty-five seconds. I could do a deadman's float for forty-five seconds. So I had just forty-five seconds left to live.

Forty seconds

No, I'd lost five seconds remembering, trying to cling to the concrete. Now I was down to forty seconds and less: thirty-nine, thirty-eight. The current from the flash flood was pushing us like rag dolls through the tunnel. I couldn't see Jeff or Tank. I couldn't see much of anything. But I felt the awful power of the water as it threw me from side to side.

Thirty-five seconds

It's not scary when you know you're going to die. I was just timing my way down, like a stopwatch counting to zero. In thirty-three seconds

I'd be dead, that was the simple fact. Someone would find my body in Mill Creek. I could even see my body floating in the river, dead and white. But what was funny was that I didn't care. I didn't care about my own death. In thirty seconds I'd be dead, it was simple. Hey, man, no worries.

Thirty seconds

Less than half a minute to go. Maybe it was being under the water that made me so dozy. They say that divers sometimes get "rapture of the deep." They throw away their scuba gear, or give their mask and fins to some friendly looking fish. And then they die. Maybe the same thing was happening to me. Maybe just before you die – when you know you're going to die – you just lose your mind. Maybe ...

Twenty-five seconds

Maybe life isn't that important. I wouldn't see Jeff anymore, but he'd be dead too. I guess Mom and Dad would feel kind of sad. Yeah, they'd be real sad, and so would Megan. In a flash I saw their faces, the looks on them. I could see the guilt they'd feel because we were dead. There'd be a funeral. Kids from school would come, and we'd be there in our coffins. Dead. Gone.

And here I was, washed away in a tunnel, not even fighting back.

Twenty seconds

Crash. My shoulder slammed into something hard and metallic, then the water pushed me right up against it. It felt like a giant hand was pressing me against this metal grate. And then it got worse. Slam, slam – I could feel my brother and Tank crash into me. Then all three of us were pressed against the grate. This must be the end, I said to myself, some kind of grate at the end of the tunnel. We're trapped between the grate and the water pushing us into it. Nobody can save us now, nobody.

Fifteen seconds

Somebody's hand is pushing around by my head. It's Jeff, trying to feel the grate or push at the grate or something. But what's the point? If the water can't push the grate open, we don't have a hope. We're going to drown like this. We're going to run out of air in our lungs and drown. It all seemed so simple. I wasn't even afraid. I'd been alive for sixteen years, mostly pretty good ones, and in twelve seconds I'd be dead. It was simple.

But then Jeff was jabbing me, grabbing my hand. He pushed my hand until I felt a little piece of metal on the grate ... an iron pin the size of my finger.

Ten seconds

What does the kid want, anyhow? There's a little piece of metal, a bolt or something. I can feel it with my hand. I can't see it, but I can feel it, kind of L-shaped like a handle or a latch. Jeff is pulling on the grate and he ... what does he want? He's trying to tell me something, jabbing at my back, putting my hand on the bolt. Why can't I figure out what he wants?

My brain feels so slow. I'm starting to run out of air, and I want to open my mouth and breathe ... but there's no way. There's no air. There's nothing but filthy water and junk all around us.

Five seconds

I was ready for the last moment, when your whole life is supposed to go before your eyes. But the last moment didn't come. Instead, my brain started working again. I figured out what Jeff wanted. He was pulling at the gate, trying to ease the pressure. But he needed me to pull the bolt. *Pull the bolt and release the gate,* I said to myself. It was simple, after all, just pull the bolt and the grate will open. *We've got one last chance. Pull the bolt and release the grate.*

CHAPTER 10

Into the Creek

The grate flew open and we shot out of there like we were blown out of a cannon. The water was already spewing around us, but when the grate let go all the garbage came with it. We went sailing into the creek with a barrage of pop cans, water bottles and tree branches.

Thank you, God, I thought to myself. *I'll never leave a water bottle on the street again, ever.*

When I got to the surface, I took a deep breath.

It was the most wonderful breath of air I had ever taken in my life. Around me, the water was surging like crazy, but it was just rough water. It wouldn't kill me. Now there was air to breathe and light to see!

"Jeff," I cried as soon as my lungs would let me.

"Over here," he shouted back. I saw him not far from my left side.

Jeff wasn't alone. He had his arm around Tank's neck, keeping the guy above the water while he swam. Somehow, Jeff had kept his promise. He had kept his buddy alive.

We swam as best we could. Mostly we let the current push us down the creek until we could get over to some land. Up ahead, off to the right, was a little muddy shore that we might just reach.

I shouted to Jeff and began swimming like crazy. I had to go sideways to the current. In a couple of seconds, I reached – or got thrown into – the beach. I crawled out on my hands and knees, feeling the sweet mud squeezing up between my fingers.

Beside me, Jeff had come up on the shore, back

first. He was still carrying Tank with his arm. I saw Jeff get up on his knees and then pull his friend out of the water.

I stopped and just caught my breath. *We're alive,* I said to myself. *We've made it.*

But my brother wasn't stopping to think or breathe. He bent down over Tank, pinched the kid's nose and began breathing into him. It was just like life-saving class, except this was real.

"Is he alive?" I asked.

Jeff said nothing. He kept breathing into Tank's mouth. Then he began pushing on his stomach. He kept it up – breathing and pushing, breathing and pushing.

Finally, Tank groaned and threw up. It was disgusting, but the guy was alive.

Up above, outside the ravine, we could hear sirens. The cops were out there, someplace, trying to find us.

"Stay with him," I told Jeff. "I'm going up to get help."

CHAPTER 11

A Hero

So what is a hero, anyway? The newspapers made a big deal about Jeff saving his friend. They wrote about the quick thinking that got the gate open just in time. There was a picture of Jeff in *The Edmonton Sun*, taking up the whole page. And my dad says the mayor is going to give him some kind of medal.

Of course, Mom and Dad are just glad we're alive. They give Jeff a lot of the credit for saving us.

And they look at me as if I were some kind of fool for going down into the sewers all by myself.

It's not fair, if you ask me. If I hadn't gone down there, Jeff and Tank would have drowned. There's no way Jeff could have pulled the pin and opened the grate himself. I saved my brother's life – and he knows it. Together we were able to save his friend, too. Still, nobody gives me credit for my role in the whole thing.

"Would you just get over it?" Megan said. Some days she sounds like Dr. Phil, handing out advice. "You're just jealous that your little brother got all the credit."

"And I got all the …" I said, ending with the usual curse.

"But Jeff was a hero," she said. "I was there with the cops. When we got down to the creek, he was still working on that guy …"

"Tank," I said, to fill the blank.

"The point is, your brother never gave up. Neither did you. In my mind, you're both heroes … except that you're the hotter guy."

It was the last part that made me blush. Megan

and I had gotten pretty close over the last couple of months. Kids at school figure we're a couple, and I guess we are. At that second, we were cuddling together on the couch – watching TV (wink, wink). Then my brother came storming down the stairs.

He saw the two of us. "Oh, sorry," he said.

"It's OK," Megan replied, sitting up nice and proper. "Larry was just telling me how much he appreciates you."

"Larry 'preciates me?" Jeff said. It was as if this were a brand new idea.

"Yeah, he says that you really were a hero back there in the storm sewer. He told me you really do deserve the mayor's medal."

Jeff's jaw dropped, almost to the floor. "Larry said that?" he asked. He was looking both at Megan and at me.

"Yeah, kind of," I said. Megan was putting words in my mouth, but they were the right words. "I'm thinking that I never really gave you enough credit back before ... the sewer thing."

"You're right," Jeff said. "You treated me like some kind of jerk."

"Well, you're still a jerk," I told him. "You're my little brother so you'll always be a jerk. But you're a hero, too. You've got a lot of things going for you that I never gave you credit for."

"Really?" Jeff asked. He was smiling, just a little.

"Yeah, you really do deserve that medal. And I'm glad that you and your gang don't hang out in the sewers anymore. Didn't I tell you that it's more fun to hang out in the ravine?"

"Yeah, I guess."

"But never mind, you're still a hero," I said. "Just don't let it go to your head."

Jeff got this enormous grin on his face, like I'd just said the nicest thing in the world.

Like I say, he's not the brightest crayon in the box. But if I ever get in trouble again – if I have to fight my way out through twenty drug dealers or two hundred deadly snakes – Jeff's the guy I want on my side.

Here are some other titles you might enjoy:

Show Off by PAUL KROPP

Nikki was one tough girl, or so all the kids said. She'd take on anybody, risk anything for the gang. But that was before she met Austin and began to turn her life around.

Ghost House by PAUL KROPP

Tyler and Zach don't believe in ghosts. So when a friend offers them big money to spend a night in the old Blackwood house, they jump at the chance. There's no such thing as ghosts, right?

Playing Chicken
by PAUL KROPP

Josh just wanted to fit in with the guys. Maybe they did a few crazy things, but that's what fun is all about. The party rolls on . . . until Guzzo dares Josh to a race that ends in death.

Caught in the Blizzard
by PAUL KROPP

Sam and Connor were enemies from the start. Sam was an Innu, close to the Arctic land that he loved. Connor was a white kid, only out for a few thrills. When a blizzard strikes, the two of them must struggle to survive in the frozen north.

Terror 9/11 by DOUG PATON

Seventeen-year-old Jason was just picking up his sister at the World Trade Centre when the first plane hit. As the towers burst into flames, he has to struggle to save his sister, his dad and himself.

Street Scene by PAUL KROPP

The guys weren't looking for trouble. Maybe Dwayne did pick the wrong girl to dance with. But did that give Sal and his gang an excuse to come after them? The fight should never have started – and it should never have finished the way it did.

Hitting the Road
by PAUL KROPP

The road isn't nice to kids who run away. Matt knew there would be trouble even before he took off with his friend Cody. Along the way, there would be fighting, fear, hunger and a jump from a speeding train. Was it all worth it?

Scarface by PAUL KROPP

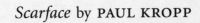

Coming to the United States had been a great thing for Tranh. This was a country of peace and wealth and happiness. So why did Martin Beamis keep picking on him? Did this rich kid have nothing better to do than make life rotten for someone who had already suffered so much?

Our Plane Is Down
by DOUG PATON

A small plane goes down in the bush, hours from anywhere. The radio is broken, the pilot is out cold. There's only a little water and even less food. Can Cal make it through the woods to save his sister, the pilot and himself?

The Kid Is Lost
by PAUL KROPP

It's a babysitter's worst nightmare: a child goes missing! Kurt has to get help and lead the search into a deadly swamp on his ATV. Will he find the lost child in time?

Student Narc
by PAUL KROPP

It wasn't Kevin's idea to start working with the cops. But when his best friend dies from an overdose, somebody has to do something. Kevin finally takes on a whole drug gang – and their boss – in a struggle that leaves him scarred for life.

Dark Ryder
by LIZ BROWN

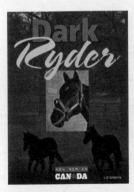

Kate Hanson finally gets the horse of her dreams, but Dark Ryder comes with a catch. Kate has just three months to turn him into a winner, or she'll lose her horse forever.

About the Author

Paul Kropp is the author of many popular novels for young people. His work includes six award-winning young-adult novels, many high-interest novels, as well as writing for adults and younger children.

Mr. Kropp's best-known novels for young adults, *Moonkid and Prometheus* and *Moonkid and Liberty*, have been translated into German, Danish, French, Portuguese and two dialects of Spanish. They have won awards both in Canada and abroad. His most recent books are *The Countess and Me* (Fitzhenry and Whiteside), a young-adult novel, and *What a Story!* (Scholastic), a picture book for young children.

Paul Kropp lives with his wife, Lori, in an 1889 townhouse in Toronto's Cabbagetown district. He has three sons (Alex, Justin and Jason) and three step-children (Emma, Ken and Jennifer).

For more information, see the author's website at
www.paulkropp.com

For more information on the books in the New Series Canada, contact:

 High Interest Publishing – Publishers of H·I·P Books
407 Wellesley Street East • Toronto, Ontario M4X 1H5
www.hip-books.com